BEASTQUEST

→← BOOK FOUR →←

TAGUS
THE NIGHT HORSE

ADAM BLADE
ILLUSTRATED BY EZRA TUCKER

A
LITTLE APPLE
PAPERBACK

SCHOLASTIC INC.

New York Toronto London Auckland
Sydney Mexico City New Delhi Hong Kong

With special thanks to Cherith Baldry

No part of this publication may be reproduced, stored in a retrieval system, or transmitted in any form or by any means, electronic, mechanical, photocopying, recording, or otherwise, without written permission of the publisher. For information regarding permission, write to Working Partners Ltd., Stanley House, St. Chad's Place, London, WC1X 9HH, United Kingdom.

ISBN-13: 978-0-439-02456-3
ISBN-10: 0-439-02456-0

Beast Quest series created by Working Partners Ltd., London.
BEAST QUEST is a registered trademark of Working Partners Ltd.

12 11   12/0

Designed by Tim Hall
Printed in the U.S.A.
First printing, September 2007

Reader,

Welcome to Avantia. I am Aduro — a good wizard residing in the palace of King Hugo. You join us at a difficult time. Let me explain. . . .

It is laid down in the Ancient Scripts that the peaceful kingdom of Avantia would one day be plunged into danger by the evil wizard, Malvel.

That time has come.

Under Malvel's evil spell, six Beasts — fire dragon, sea serpent, mountain giant, night horse, ice beast, and winged flame — run wild and destroy the land they once protected.

The kingdom is in great danger.

The Scripts also predict an unlikely hero. They say that a boy shall take up the Quest to free the beasts and save the kingdom.

We hope this young boy will take up the Quest. Will you join us as we wait and watch?

Avantia salutes you,
Aduro

VICTOR AWOKE WITH A START. GRABBING HIS sword, he sat up and looked around wildly. It was just before dawn and the sky was beginning to lighten in the east. The coals from last night's campfire were still glowing red. Victor surveyed the plain — nothing seemed out of the ordinary.

Must have been a bad dream, he thought to himself as he settled back onto his bedroll.

But sleep was the last thing on Victor's mind. In the last couple of weeks, three separate attacks had struck the cattle drives. None of the cattlemen were getting much sleep at night.

No one knew who was behind the attacks, but according to the rumors, a horseman was responsible. Victor didn't know what to think, but one thing was for sure: He was glad the night was almost over.

Lying on his bedroll, Victor listened to the sounds of the plains. There was a slight breeze rustling the tall prairie grasses and he could hear the last of the crickets chirping softly. Then, a bird called out over the lowing cattle.

Something wasn't right. The cattle should be sleeping. Propping himself up on his elbows, he looked toward the horizon. The cattle were huddled together more tightly than usual, with their calves grouped in the center — a sign that they felt threatened. But by what?

Victor thought he could make out the sound of hooves drumming in the distance. Was it just his imagination?

The cattle began mooing frantically. Victor rose to his feet and stood by the fire's coals as the sound of hoofbeats drew nearer.

There, in the red glow of the coals, he saw the

mysterious horseman. Victor gasped. This was no ordinary horseman! This was something much more horrifying — the torso of a giant man, attached to the body of a powerful stallion. Stumbling backward in fear, Victor stared up at the huge half man–half horse. His dark hair and beard were wildly tangled and the reflection from the campfire had turned his eyes a flaming red.

The creature reared up on its hind legs, grunting fiercely, its hooves pounding the air. The Beast was ready to charge!

Victor tried to dive out of the way. But he wasn't fast enough. One of the Beast's hooves struck him on the head, knocking him to the ground. The Beast galloped through the fire, scattering the red-hot coals in a flurry of sparks. It flung its head back and roared as the dry grass began to catch fire.

Dazed, Victor saw the creature charge toward the helpless cattle. Before he could do anything, the pain overcame him and everything went black.

CHAPTER ONE

A Thousand Hooves

"I THINK THAT WAS THE BIGGEST CHALLENGE yet," said Tom.

He sat tall in the saddle as he rode down the hills from the north of Avantia on his black horse, Storm. His friend Elenna rode behind him, her arms around his waist. Tom had just released Cypher the giant from the evil spell of the wizard Malvel. They were all tired from the struggle, but Storm kept going. Silver, the wolf, padded quietly after them.

"I thought I'd be trapped in that cave forever," Elenna agreed. "Cypher was so angry!"

"I'd be angry, too, if an evil wizard had enslaved

me!" Tom said. He gave a sigh of satisfaction. "But Cypher is free now. There will be no more trouble."

"Not from him," Elenna pointed out. "But we have a new Beast Quest now. How long do you think it will take to reach the plains?"

"It's not far," said Tom. "I hope we're ready for it, that's all." He reached out and touched the saddlebag holding his sword and was reminded of all the challenges he had faced so far.

"I know you have it in you," Elenna said, giving him a playful jab. "And don't forget, you've got me to protect you."

Tom glanced over his shoulder and smiled. "I haven't forgotten. I'm glad we met in the forest."

It was early morning and the sun had just risen. Tom brought Storm to a halt and pulled out his magical map from one of the saddlebags. Elenna peered over his shoulder so she could see it, too. A glowing red line showed the road from the mountain town of Colton to the plain of Dareton in the middle of the kingdom. Tiny cattle moved about on the plain, eating the rich grass.

"I think we're about here." Tom pointed to the edge of the hills on the map. "It can't be too far now."

"Can you see Dareton?" Elenna asked, moving to get a better view of the map. "That's the main town, isn't it?"

"There," Tom pointed, "that's where we're headed." He put the map away and looked at the plains below them. He could see the long grasses swaying in the breeze. With a nudge of his heels, he urged Storm onward. "Since we're getting close, we should keep an eye out for the next Beast."

"Wizard Aduro said he's half man, half horse," Elenna said, shivering.

Tom nodded. "Tagus. He's attacking the cattle on the plain. The people of Dareton could starve."

Tom tightened his grip on the reins. He knew

how important it was to free Tagus from the evil enchantment. Storm nickered, as if he knew what they were up against. Tom patted his horse's neck. With each Quest, their bond grew stronger.

They came to the crest of a low hill. Tom looked out across the wide plain that stretched as far as he could see. A river wound through clumps of trees and gently sloping hills. In the distance, a lake glinted in the sunlight. Silver's ears pricked up and he sniffed the air eagerly.

"It's beautiful!" Elenna exclaimed. "Maybe Aduro sent us here before Tagus had the chance to do terrible damage."

"Could be." Tom's heartbeat quickened with hope. In the south, the crops had been burned by dragon fire. In the west, Sepron the sea serpent had flooded the coast. Cypher the giant had destroyed the northern hills with rock slides. Tom had almost forgotten what ordinary, peaceful countryside looked like. "Look over there," he said, pointing into the distance. He could just make out square gray towers and rooftops covered with red tiles. "That must be Dareton."

"Then let's go!" said Elenna.

Storm cantered down the hill toward the plain. Tom enjoyed the steady beat of his hooves, sensing his horse's rising excitement. Silver let out a joyful yelp and bounded ahead of them. He disappeared into the long grass until all Tom and Elenna could see of him was the tip of his tail.

On the breeze Tom could smell a hint of smoke, as if there was a campfire burning nearby. He scanned the horizon to see if he could catch sight of it. Looking south across the plain, Tom spotted a herd of cattle. Moving in a thick mass, the herd appeared to be heading toward them.

"That's odd," Tom said. "Shouldn't the cattle be moving toward Dareton?"

As they watched from Storm's saddle, Tom and Elenna sensed that something was wrong.

The herd wasn't walking peacefully. They were stampeding!

"We have to get out of here," Tom said. "They're heading right for us!"

"Silver!" Elenna called to her wolf. She let out a piercing whistle, and within seconds the gray wolf was bounding through the tall grass toward them.

"Good boy," Tom said, looking east toward Dareton. If they could move quickly enough, they might be able to get out of the stampede's way and reach safety. Tom squeezed Storm's flanks and the horse took off through the prairie grass toward town.

Running at full speed, Storm cut across the plain like a bolt of lightning. Silver followed at their heels. But they couldn't get out of the way of the stampeding herd. Dust had begun to fill the air and the sound of their hooves pounding the hard ground was deafening.

When Storm crested onto a slight rise in the ground, Tom caught a glimpse of the cattle. The herd was much larger then he had thought. There must have been a thousand animals, each the size of a large boulder. They were charging through the plain, trampling flat anything in their way.

The ground was shaking under the weight of the massive animals. Tom could feel Elenna squeezing him tightly as they flew across the plains toward Dareton. They were almost out of the way of the stampede when Storm skidded to a stop.

"Go, Storm! Keep going!" Tom yelled, kicking at the horse's flanks. "We're almost there —"

Tom heard a crackling sound and looked up. Instantly, he knew why Storm had stopped so suddenly. Just in front of them, a raging fire was consuming the tall, dry grass of the prairie.

CHAPTER TWO

TRAPPED!

THEY WERE TRAPPED. THE RAMPAGING CATTLE were closing in and there was nowhere to go. The only thing they could do was run with the stampede. This would be risky, but they had no choice.

Tom wheeled Storm around, and the brave horse began running alongside the cattle. Before they knew it, Tom and Elenna were surrounded by a raging sea of stampeding animals.

Choking on the dust and smoke, Tom urged Storm to run faster. "Go, boy! Go!"

After a quarter of a mile, they had outrun the spreading fire.

"Quick, go left!" Tom yelled, pulling on Storm's reins. The horse made an abrupt turn, breaking from the stampede. Tom eased him to a stop.

"We need to make a firebreak, to stop the fire from reaching Dareton!" Tom yelled above the thundering hooves. "I'll need my sword and shield!"

Tom jumped down from Storm's back as Elenna handed him his shield and weapon. Running toward the approaching flames, Tom began chopping the tall grass with his sword. He knew if he could clear a wide enough break in front of the fire's path, it would have nowhere to go.

Running and chopping, Tom cleared a large swath of grass. The dragon scale in his shield kept him safe from the blaze. He did it again and again until the flames had nothing left to consume and began to die down.

As the fire flickered out, Tom collapsed to the ground in exhaustion. His face was covered in soot and he was coughing from all the smoke he had inhaled.

"Let's rest a bit before moving on," Elenna suggested, handing Tom some water and a little food. "Storm could use a break, too."

Tom walked a little ways to survey the damage. But he didn't want to stay put for long. "We'd better get moving soon," he called to Elenna as soon as he'd finished his bread. "The town will have stables where Storm can rest properly."

Just then, a shout rang out. "There he is!"

Tom looked up to see a band of men approaching from the direction of Dareton. Tom was glad he had stopped the fire before it reached the town.

"Hurry, let's get him!" another man shouted.

As the men approached, Tom knew something wasn't right. These men weren't here to thank him — they were angry and carrying weapons. Tom gripped his sword and shield tightly.

"Elenna, leave them to me," Tom told his friend

as the mob drew nearer. "Take Storm and Silver to safety." He watched as Elenna mounted Storm and galloped away, with Silver at her side. She cast him a worried look, but Tom did his best to look calm.

The crowd surrounded him. They were all big men, brandishing scythes and pitchforks. Their faces glared red with rage. But at least they hadn't seen his friends get away.

There were too many of them to fight. And Tom didn't understand why they were so angry — all he'd done was save their town from a wildfire. He took a step back as they jostled one another, trying to grab him.

"Wait a minute. I haven't done anything wrong —" Tom began.

No one listened to him. One of the men pushed forward and grabbed Tom by the shoulder. "Where's Victor?" he demanded.

Everyone seemed to be shouting at once. "Look

at him — covered in soot! He must have started the fire."

"And what about our cattle?" Another man thrust his face close to Tom's, glaring fiercely at him. "You've caused them to stampede."

Someone else struck Tom a powerful blow on the back that knocked the air from him. "Our families will starve!"

"Who's Victor? I don't know what you're talking about," Tom sputtered, trying to get his wind back. "I put out the fire! I didn't start the stampede!"

But the men were yelling, and Tom couldn't make himself heard. Fear surged up inside him as they crowded around. He gripped his sword tightly, but one of the men wrenched it out of his hands.

Then another voice rang out. "Wait! Let me talk to him." A tall man pushed his way to the front of the crowd. He had dark hair and a stern face. "Calm down," he ordered. "I'll soon find out what's going on."

The crowd moved back a bit and their shouts died down to angry muttering.

"I'm Adam, the head guard of Dareton," the tall man said. "My son, Victor, disappeared from a cattle drive last night. Do you know anything about him?"

Tom's heart pounded as he looked at the angry faces staring at him. "No, I'm sorry," he said. "I've only just come down from the north. I barely escaped the stampede myself. I'm the one that put out the fire." He glanced around at the circle of suspicious faces and added, "You've got to let me go. I have something important to do."

"I'll bet!" one of the men jeered. He reached out and grabbed Tom's arm. Someone else grabbed his other arm.

"So you won't tell the truth, eh?" a voice called out. "We'll see about that! Take him to the jail!"

⤙ CHAPTER THREE ⤚

BEHIND BARS

By the time Tom and his captors reached Dareton, the sun had set. The streets were dark and narrow, with overhanging roofs that hid the sky. Rubbish lay scattered around the market stalls and stray dogs picked among the scraps.

Adam and the other guards marched Tom through the streets, with the rest of the men following close on their heels. Tom tried to pull away from the rough grip of his captors, but it was no use. These men were twice his size, and strong.

"Why won't you listen to me?" Tom pleaded. "I don't know anything about your son."

"Then tell me, why are you here?" Adam asked

him. "And what's so important about what you have to do?"

"I can't tell you that," he answered. Tom knew he had to keep his Beast Quest secret.

"If that's the way you want it," said Adam. It was clear his patience was running thin.

The band of men stopped outside a big stone building. Two guards stood by the door. Tom began to panic as he realized where he was.

"No!" he exclaimed. "You can't put me in there."

Still keeping a firm grip on Tom's shoulder, Adam turned to face the men. "Go back to your homes," he ordered. "I'll see that justice is done."

"Make sure that you do!" someone yelled from the back of the crowd.

"Don't worry about that. If the boy knows anything about Victor, I'll find out."

The crowd shuffled away, giving Tom angry looks as they went.

"This is for your own protection, too," Adam

said. "Those men are desperate. They might kill you if given the chance."

He pushed open the door and thrust Tom inside. One of the guards followed.

Tom was standing in a large, bare room lit by an oil lamp hanging from a beam. In the middle of the room was an old wooden table and chair. No one else was there. The guard pushed Tom across the room and through an inner door into a long, stone-flagged passage. On either side of the hall were heavy iron doors. Tom felt his stomach tighten with fear.

The guard unhooked a bunch of keys from his belt and opened the door. Then he grabbed Tom by the arm and threw him inside. Tom sprawled onto the filth of the cell floor, then climbed awkwardly to his feet, rubbing his elbow.

"I'll question you in the morning," said Adam gruffly. "A night in the cells should loosen your tongue."

The cell door slammed shut and the guard turned the key. The two men walked away, their footsteps muffled by the heavy door.

Tom looked around his cell. The walls and floor were stone and there were no windows. Along one wall was a wooden bench with a single, tattered blanket. Tom shivered and tried not to breathe in too much of the foul smell.

Now what do I do? he wondered. He couldn't save Avantia from Tagus the Night Horse if he was locked up in this cell!

"You there!"

The sound of a hoarse voice made Tom spin around. He put his ear to the door but couldn't hear anything.

"No — down here."

Tom scanned the cell carefully. Under the bench in the shadows was a small hole covered by bars. Tom got down on his hands and knees and looked through the opening.

"What are you here for?" the prisoner asked. "Thieving? Young lads are always thieving."

"I'm not a thief!" Tom retorted. "It's all a mistake. I shouldn't be here at all."

The prisoner let out a rusty laugh. "That's what we all say."

"But it's true!" Tom said, his voice tense with frustration. "The guard and some other men arrested me out on the plain. They think I've got something to do with the guard's son disappearing, but I never even saw him."

The prisoner nodded. "Riding a horse were you?"

"Yes, but why —?"

"A horseman has been causing a lot of trouble hereabouts."

Tom was suddenly alert. "What sort of trouble?" he asked, wondering how much the townspeople already knew.

"Lurking on the plains at night," the prisoner replied, a hint of excitement in his voice. "Attacking cattle and causing stampedes. Two towns have already been destroyed — trampled flat."

"But who is he?" Tom asked.

"Nobody knows. He comes at night, and nobody ever gets a good look at him. They just hear his horse's hoofbeats."

Tom was certain that the stranger was telling him about Tagus. No one had seen the invader clearly; they thought he was an ordinary horseman, not a creature that was half man and half horse.

"But why me?" Tom asked. "I'm only a boy, after all."

The prisoner shrugged. "People are always wary of strangers."

Tom opened his mouth to protest again, but stopped himself. He knew that the troubles in Dareton were all the work of the Beast. But he couldn't explain that, not to this prisoner. Tom had to get out!

⊶ CHAPTER FOUR ⊷

HOOFBEATS IN THE NIGHT

T OM PACED AROUND THE CELL. *There has to be a way out*, he thought. Patting the stones against the outside wall with an open palm, Tom listened carefully. If there were any weak spots, there would be a hollow sound instead of a slap. Tom checked all the stones he could reach, but they were all solid.

Next, Tom inspected the grout holding the stones together. It was a mixture of dried tar and rock flakes — impossible to chip away without a chisel. Tom sat down on the bench feeling helpless.

"You hungry, boy?" came the gravelly voice from the next cell.

"No," Tom replied coldly. This was not the time to be thinking about food. He had to find a way out. Then an idea hit him. If he could get the guard to bring some food, the door would have to be opened, if only for a moment.

Tom walked over and examined the door. The lock was well built: A bolt slid from the door and into a hole in the wall when the key was turned. As he leaned in closer, Tom's train of thought was interrupted by a drop of water. And another. What was it? He looked up, and sure enough, a steady drip came from the ceiling above. He glanced back at the lock. An old leak had worn a gap between the wall and the door — just wide enough for Tom's fingers to slip through. Tom tapped at the stone. It wasn't very strong. It had been weakened by months or years of constant dripping. If Tom could stuff something into the hole when the guard unlocked the door . . .

Tom tore a strip of cloth from his shirt as

he thought over his plan. He knew he would have to be quick. It would be a matter of seconds — even less, perhaps — between the guard unlocking the door and opening it. Going over his plan, Tom tried to visualize what he had to do. The moment the door was unlocked, he would stuff the fabric against the side of the hole. Then, when the guard bolted the door again, the bolt would force the fabric against the stone. With any luck, the force would be just enough to crumble the weakened rock.

When he felt sure he could do it, he called out to the guard.

"Hello — Hello —" Tom yelled as loud as he could. He listened as the guard's heavy footsteps came down the corridor.

"What is it, boy?" he asked roughly.

"I'm hungry," Tom called out.

"Then you'll have to wait till morning," the guard said cruelly.

"But I haven't eaten in days!" Tom hated lying, but he had no choice. He had to get out.

"Then eat your shoe!" The guard laughed, clearly taking pleasure in being mean.

"You have to feed me," Tom yelled back. "It's the law of Avantia that you treat prisoners with dignity!"

Tom listened as the footsteps disappeared down the corridor. He waited with his ear to the door. Hopefully the guard had some decency.

A few moments later, Tom heard the guard coming back down the corridor. Tom readied himself, placing his fingers in the space between the door and the wall. The footsteps stopped before the door and Tom heard the guard fiddling with the keys. This was it!

Tom felt the lock bolt slide back into the door as the guard turned the key. As quick as he could, he pushed the cloth against the side of the hole. Just as he stuffed it in, the door swung open and struck him heavily in the forehead, sending him flying.

The guard stomped in as Tom lay sprawled on the ground.

"Trying to escape, eh?" the guard laughed, looking down at Tom. "There's no escaping from here, lad."

Tom looked up at the guard, his vision blurry from the blow to his head. The guard was smiling a cruel, crooked-toothed grin. Then he dropped a plate of cold gruel on the stone floor and stomped out of the cell, pulling the door closed behind him. As the guard turned the lock, Tom heard the faint clink of pebbles against the floor of the cell.

It had worked! But Tom waited until the footsteps had disappeared before daring to move toward the front of the cell. When he was sure the guard had gone, he pulled gently on the door. The rest of the stone crumbled around the bolt, and the door opened.

Tom cautiously peeked his head out and checked that no guards had appeared. Satisfied that the coast was clear, he stepped into the hallway and shut the door behind him. Then he crept down the passage toward the door at the end.

Tom put his ear to the door and listened. Everything was silent. At last he dared to edge the door open a crack and peer through. The room was in darkness. No guards were there.

Tom slid into the room and closed the door behind him. Then he froze. The latch on the outer door was being lifted. Tom darted for the only hiding place he could see, a dark archway in one wall. The door swung open and the guard appeared. "I'll just check on the prisoners," he said, glancing over his shoulder.

He tramped across the room and through the door to the cells. Tom's stomach lurched. Tom only had a few minutes before the guard would discover that he was missing! He had to hurry. But there were still several more guards between Tom and the front door. He couldn't get out that way.

Tom saw he was standing at the foot of a spiral staircase. He had no idea where the stone steps led, but it was the only way to go. He climbed up, clutching the rope looped along the wall.

Groping in the darkness, Tom felt a wooden frame in the stone wall. He realized it must be a window. The shutters were closed; Tom fumbled with the catch until he could swing them open.

Just then the guard called out. "The boy is gone!" Tom could hear the other guards shouting frantically. "Over here! Maybe he went up here!" Tom heard the guards start up the staircase. He had to get out.

In the moonlight, Tom saw that the tall window led out onto a small balcony — a guard's post. He rushed to the rail and peered down to the street. There were no guards in sight; this must be the back of the prison.

He had hoped he would be able to climb down,

but the wall was sheer. There was nothing he could hold on to. "Now what?" he asked himself.

He had to get down fast. He would have to risk climbing over the rail and letting himself drop into the street. He didn't dare think what would happen if he broke a leg. Tom wished he still had his shield. Since he freed Cypher, the shield had the power to protect him when jumping or falling from great heights. But the guards had taken it, and Tom had no idea what they had done with it.

He was gripping the rail, ready to swing himself over, when he heard a sound slicing through the darkness. His heart almost stopped. Slow hoofbeats echoed in the silence of the night. They were getting louder.

What had the other prisoner said about the mysterious horseman who attacked in the night? All anyone ever heard of him was the sound of hoofbeats —

Could it be Tagus?

CHAPTER FIVE

VICTOR

THE HOOFBEATS WERE GETTING CLOSER. Would Tagus dare come into the town?

Tom crouched behind the rail and peered down into the street again. A shape appeared out of the shadows. Tom sagged with relief as he recognized the horse and its rider. It was Elenna and Storm!

"Elenna —" he called softly.

Elenna halted the horse just below the balcony and looked up. "Tom. Are you all right?" she whispered back.

"I'm fine. Just help me get out of here."

Elenna unfastened a rope from the saddle. It was

the one they used to tie up Storm. "Catch," she said, tossing it to him.

Tom grabbed the end and tied it around the balcony rail. Then he hesitated, looking back through the window. Somewhere inside, the guards had his sword and shield.

"Come on," Elenna urged him.

Tom knew he had no choice. He swung himself over the balcony rail just as the guards appeared at the window.

"There he is! Get him!" they called out as he climbed down the rope, dropping neatly onto Storm's back.

"*Go!*" he yelled.

As they rode through the darkness, Elenna told Tom how worried she had been.

"After they took you, I didn't know what to do," she said. "I took Storm and Silver to the lake and

made a camp. I was so worried for you. But I knew I should wait until dark to come help."

"You came at just the right time," Tom said. "I couldn't have escaped without you."

The prairie was quiet and still. It was a clear night and the moon and stars gave enough light for them to make their way back to the camp.

Tom looked over his shoulder. "I think we've lost them," he said, relieved.

"It's not much farther," Elenna said. They could see the surface of the lake shimmering in the moonlight.

Nearing the camp, Storm slowed down to a trot. In the quiet of the night, they heard a whimper. Elenna halted Storm. Tom scanned the darkness, listening closely. The sound continued. It was coming from a thicket of bushes up ahead.

Tom scrambled down from Storm and rushed over to the thicket. Elenna followed, leading Storm by the reins. Lying on the ground was a boy. "Who are you?" Tom asked.

"M-m-my name's Victor," the boy stuttered, clearly in pain.

"Victor!" Tom shouted. "Are you Adam's son?" Victor nodded. Tom couldn't believe it! "I've seen your father. He's been looking everywhere for you."

"I was helping with the cattle drive," Victor explained. He swallowed, clenching his fists as if he was remembering something terrible. "We'd all heard the stories about the horseman who kept attacking the cattle. Last night I was keeping watch, and I saw him."

"You saw him?" Elenna exclaimed, squatting down beside Victor.

"Yes, but he wasn't just a horseman," Victor replied, staring into the flames. "When I was young, my mother told me about Tagus the Night Horse, who keeps watch over the herds. I always thought that was just a story, like the rest of the Beasts. It sounds unbelievable, but I saw him — half man and half horse. But he wasn't there to protect us. I was terrified! He reared up and one of his hooves hit me and knocked me over. He scattered the coals from the campfire and roared as the dry grass began to burn. Then he charged toward the cattle! I tried to get up, but I felt dizzy. Everything went black. When I woke up, there was a huge fire and the cattle were stampeding. I ran, trying to get away. But I tripped and fell. I think I broke my leg." Victor winced, touching his leg gingerly.

Tom looked at Elenna. Victor was lucky to be alive. Tagus was out of control. They didn't have much time to free the Beast from the evil spell. During the next attack, someone could be seriously hurt — or even killed.

"Here," Tom said, helping the boy up onto his good leg. Together they hobbled the short distance to the camp Elenna had made. Once there, Tom laid out a bedroll for Victor while Elenna prepared some fish she had caught earlier.

As the fish cooked over the small campfire, Tom examined Victor's leg. It didn't look good. His whole leg was swollen and bruised, and Victor flinched in pain at even the slightest touch. Tom gave him some water and kept talking to him, trying to keep Victor's mind off his injury.

When the fish was ready, Elenna divided the portions among the three of them.

"You should eat something," Elenna said to Victor. "It will help." Victor tried to swallow a few bites, but he was in too much pain to eat.

"We'll have to go back to Dareton first thing in the morning," Tom said to Elenna. "Victor needs care, but it's too dangerous to travel at night with Tagus on the loose."

Tom swallowed the last of the fish and settled down on his blanket next to Elenna and Victor. Storm was sleeping on his feet behind them and

Silver had curled up next to Elenna. They were all exhausted. Tom peered out into the darkness. Nothing. He climbed under his blanket and tried to sleep. But the sounds of the plain were unfamiliar and kept him awake. The long grasses rustled in the night breeze and crickets chirped to one another. Then there was another sound. A low moaning carried over the land that made Tom shiver. He sat up sharply and listened. There it was again! But this time the moan sounded angry — ready for battle.

Tom shook Elenna awake.

"Did you hear that?" he whispered. The two of them listened, but heard nothing out of the ordinary. Elenna shook her head, still half asleep, and settled back down.

"Get some sleep," she muttered.

Tom waited and listened for a while longer. But whatever it was had gone. Could it have been Tagus? There was nothing Tom could do in the dark. He would have to wait for morning.

→ CHAPTER SIX ←

THE CATTLE DRIVE

Dawn light spread across the plain as Tom and Elenna packed up their camp.

"There's no time for breakfast," Tom said grimly, as he and Elenna lifted Victor onto Storm's saddle. "We need to get going — now." He couldn't say why things were so urgent in front of Victor, but the boy's condition wasn't good and they had to get him to a doctor as soon as possible. Victor was slipping in and out of consciousness and was barely able to talk.

They reached Dareton as the sun rose. Tom was riding Storm with Victor slumped in the saddle in front of him, while Elenna walked alongside with Silver. It was early — the streets should have been empty. But there were clusters of townspeople whispering amongst themselves. Some people were openly weeping. Tom pulled Storm to a halt.

"What is it?" he asked one of the groups. "What's wrong?" A young man turned and peered up at Tom, shielding his eyes against the early morning sun. He looked so angry that Tom wondered what he would do.

"Another herd of cattle stampeded in the night," the young man said. He spat on the ground in disgust.

Just as the young man was about to walk away, another man called out. "There he is!"

All at once, the townspeople turned and looked at Tom.

"And he's got Victor!" called out another. Before Tom knew it, he was surrounded by an angry mob. Men were waving weapons and yelling at the top of their lungs.

Hearing the commotion, a guard approached the crowd. Seeing Tom, he drew his sword and called to the other guards at the prison. "It's the boy who's been causing the stampedes."

Someone grabbed Storm's reins and another pulled Victor from the saddle. Victor let out a cry of pain. Before he had a chance to flee, Tom, too, was dragged from Storm's back. The crowd was so worked up that Tom expected things to turn violent at any moment.

"What's going on here?" came a gruff voice from the edge of the mob. Things quieted down as Adam made his way to Tom.

"It's the boy that escaped," a guard said. "And he's got your son."

Adam looked at Victor lying in the dirt. A woman was trying to comfort him as he writhed and winced. Adam then turned to Tom, his eyes narrowing in fierce anger.

"What have you done?" he thundered. "What have you done to my boy?"

As Adam drew his sword, a weak voice sounded next to Tom. It was Victor.

"Wait —" Victor's voice was choked with pain. "It's not Tom's fault. Tom didn't cause the stampedes. He saved me."

A murmur went through the crowd.

The townspeople were silent as they looked at Adam for his reaction.

"Release the boy," he said. "And someone get the doctor."

Victor's father then looked at Tom. "I'm sorry," he said. "I was wrong to lock you up." He looked out at the crowd of people and their worried faces. "We've had other things to worry about since then," he added quietly. He held out a hand and Tom shook it. "You deserve a reward," he went on. "Ask for whatever you want. You brought my son back."

"I don't want a reward," Tom replied, "just my sword and shield."

Adam nodded to one of the guards, who dashed into the prison and then reappeared carrying the sword and shield. He gave them to Tom.

"Thank you," Tom said. He fitted the sword into its sheath and slung the shield over his shoulder. Now he was ready to face Tagus.

"So, why are you here?" Adam asked. "Have you come to stay in Dareton?"

"No." It was Elenna who replied, stepping forward to stand beside Tom. "We've been visiting the mountains in the north, and now we're on our way home."

Tom felt his shoulder being tapped. He turned to see the guard who had been so mean the night before. His face looked friendly now. "You'll need food for your journey," he said, holding out a loaf of bread. "Take this. We're sorry we didn't believe you."

Tom was glad he had been cleared. But he still didn't know how to find Tagus. Then, something occurred to Tom. Maybe he wouldn't have to go after the Beast — maybe the Beast would find him.

"Let us help you on the next cattle drive," Tom suggested to the townspeople. "If you have more people to keep watch, you might have a better chance of keeping them safe." He exchanged a glance with Elenna.

"That's a generous offer," Adam said. "But it's risky. I don't know if we ought to ask you. . . ."

"We have to go home. And we'll be safer with the cattle drive than traveling alone," Elenna pointed out. "At least we can start our journey with you."

A broad, red-faced man pushed his way to the front of the crowd. "My name's Samuel," he announced. "Me and my neighbor, Jacob, are taking our cattle south tomorrow. It's the biggest drive of the season — we're going to the palace to sell the cattle at market. We'll be glad for your help." He paused, giving Silver a doubtful look. "That's a powerful big dog you've got there. It is a dog, isn't it?" he added nervously.

"He's a wolf," said Elenna cheerfully. "But don't worry. He's well trained. He won't harm your cattle."

"Maybe he'll sink his teeth into the horseman," said a voice from the crowd.

"Let's hope he does," Samuel agreed, grinning with relief.

Adam nodded, as if he had made up his mind. "Then it's settled," he said to Tom and Elenna. "You'll leave tomorrow at dawn."

The next morning, Adam guided Tom and Elenna to the edge of town. The cattle drive was ready to set out. A crowd of townspeople had gathered to see them off. Yapping dogs dashed up and down, and children called out excitedly.

Tom gazed in amazement at the huge number

of cattle milling about on the plain. The air was filled with the sound of their lowing and the soft clang of the bells around their necks.

Slowly the herd of cattle began to move off. Some were huge beasts with shaggy black coats and curving horns. Others were young calves, trotting along beside their mothers.

Horsemen rode alongside the herd on either side. Children from the town ran after them. "Good-bye!" they called. "Good luck!"

"Good-bye! Take care!"

Tom found a place near the back of the herd. At home in his village, he had often thought it would be fun to join one of the great cattle drives from Dareton. Now he had his wish, and he wasn't thinking about having fun at all. He just wanted to see the herd safely on its way, and to find Tagus and release him from Malvel's evil spell.

The walls and towers of Dareton disappeared behind them. Tom began to get used to the smell and the noise of the cattle. Silver was running along the edge of the herd, drawing ahead and then bounding back with yelps of excitement. Some of the calves shied away nervously.

"Silver loves this!" Elenna exclaimed.

As she spoke, the wolf darted after a cow that had wandered away. He overtook it and turned to face it, throwing back his head to howl. The cow rolled its eyes and galloped back to the herd with the wolf behind it.

Tom laughed. "He seems to know what he's doing!"

As the day went on, the cattle became used to Silver. They moved at the same slow pace, dust swirling around their hooves. The air was full of the sound of their lowing.

Tom kept scanning the horizon, but he couldn't

see any sign of Tagus. Then he caught sight of deep hoof prints in a damp patch of ground. "Look!" he said to Elenna. "Tagus has been here."

Elenna frowned. "It could be one of the cattlemen's horses."

"No — these prints are huge!" Tom shivered. "I think the Beast must be close by."

The sun was going down when the herd gradually slowed to a halt. Tom realized that the cattle in the lead must have stopped.

"We're making camp," Samuel told them as he rode by. "There's a river up ahead where the cattle can drink."

Urging Storm on, Tom and Elenna skirted the edge of the herd until they reached the river. A muddy slope, churned up by many hooves, led down to the water. Here and there, the cattle drivers were beginning to make campfires.

"Let's make our fire over there," Elenna suggested, pointing upstream to where trees grew close to the water's edge. "We can keep an eye out for Tagus."

"Good idea," Tom agreed.

Tom and Elenna made their way upstream. Beyond the trees the ground sloped upward and the lush grass of the plain gave way to bare rock.

He and Elenna made a fire at the edge of the river; the leaping scarlet flames glowed in the twilight. Tom peered past the flames and out across the plain. But there was no sign of the horseman. Not yet. Elenna pulled bread and cheese out of one of Storm's saddlebags. She broke a loaf in two and gave one half to Tom.

"The people in Dareton were really generous with their food," she said. "If this cattle drive gets attacked, too, they'll be without enough for themselves. They've already lost so much. We *have* to help them."

"We will," said Tom. "We'll free Tagus, whatever it takes."

Night fell and Tom could hardly make out the herd among the shadows. The darkness was dotted with the red glow of other campfires.

"One of us will have to stay awake," Elenna said. "You try to get some sleep, and I'll take the first watch."

"All right." Tom pulled his blanket around himself and lay down by the fire. "Don't forget to wake me."

"Tom — Tom —"

Someone was tugging at Tom's shoulder. He opened his eyes to see Elenna's face just above him.

"Everything's quiet," Elenna whispered. "And it's your turn to keep watch now." She gave an enormous yawn. "I can't stay awake any longer."

"All right, I'm up." Tom walked over to the riverbank and splashed his face with water to wake himself up.

Elenna built up the fire and then lay down

beside it. "Wake me if you hear anything," she murmured.

Tom scrambled up the tallest tree and found a fork in the branches where he could sit and look out over the plain. A half-moon was shining through thin clouds. Beyond the camp, nothing disturbed the darkness.

Hours went by, but Tom still saw nothing. The sky in the east grew pale as dawn approached. The danger seemed to be over for another night. But Tom was desperate to find Tagus. When would he appear? Every muscle in Tom's body was tensed with anticipation.

Tom was about to climb down from the tree when he spotted a black outline where the sky was the brightest — right on the other side of the river.

"Tagus!" Tom whispered under his breath. At last!

It was a powerful figure, half man, half horse. As Tom stared, the creature reared, hooves striking out at the air. A battle cry louder than Tom had ever heard before echoed across the plain. Tagus began to gallop toward the camp.

But Tagus attacks only at night! Tom's stomach tightened and he gripped the branch. If Tagus was now attacking during the day, it meant he was growing bolder. He obviously didn't care about keeping himself hidden.

Tom swung himself off the branch and dropped to the ground beside the campfire. Tom felt a rush of adrenaline. This was the moment he'd been waiting for. He could feel the ground vibrating as Tagus pounded toward the herd. Tom drew his sword. "Elenna! Elenna!" he called.

Elenna sat up, pushing her hair out of her eyes. "What's the matter?"

"Tagus is coming," Tom said. "This is it. We're going to face him, *now*."

CHAPTER SEVEN

TAGUS BOUND

"WE HAVE TO HEAD TAGUS OFF," TOM WENT on. "We can't risk him getting near the herd."

Elenna sprang to her feet and followed Tom as he skirted the edge of the camp. Silver padded at their heels. They quietly passed Samuel's campfire. The cattleman was wrapped up in a thick blanket. Elenna stooped to pick up a coil of rope from near the fire and slung it over her shoulder. "Which way?" she asked Tom.

Tom gazed out across the plain. Tagus had disappeared from view, but Tom knew he must be near. He strained to pick up the sound of hoofbeats, but all he could hear were the soft sounds of drowsy cattle.

Then the mist parted and Tagus appeared. The Beast was on the other side of the river, hooves pawing the ground in a fury. His muscles rippled beneath the shiny black coat of his horse's body. He flicked his tail in agitation. His face was handsome, and he had curly black hair and a beard. Tom could see that Tagus was ready to attack and was only waiting for the right moment. There was no time to waste.

Tom gripped his sword and stepped toward the river's edge. His stomach churned in fear at the thought of those pounding hooves.

"No!" Elenna clutched at his arm and dragged him into the shelter of a jutting rock. "Maybe we should wait for him to come to us."

"We can't," Tom said. "If we let him cross the river, he'll be close enough to attack. We need to stop him from crossing."

"But how?" Elenna asked, a worried look on her face.

"I've got an idea," Tom said bravely. "Give me the rope. I'll ride out with Storm."

Tom grabbed Storm's reins and hoisted himself onto the saddle, leaving Elenna and Silver to keep watch. He hated to bring his horse into battle, but it was necessary. It was the only way he could cross the river quickly enough. Storm gave a nervous whinny and Tom patted his mane.

"I know, boy, I'm scared, too," Tom said, reassuring his horse. "But I know you can do it. You outran Ferno the Fire Dragon, and now I need you to outrun Tagus."

Storm reared up and charged toward the river. As he plunged into the water, Tom gasped. The water was ice-cold and moving fast. Storm fought his way across, but the current was strong and pulled them downriver. Tom watched Tagus on the other side. The Beast was pacing back and forth, like a lion waiting for its prey. Tom felt fear wash over him.

As Storm neared the river's bank, Tom tied a quick slipknot on one end of his rope. Tom focused on Tagus's collar. It gave off a soft glow, and was secured with a lock, just like the others had been. With any luck, he could lasso the Beast and subdue him long enough to break Malvel's enchantment.

Storm panted heavily as they reached firm ground. Crossing the river had taken a lot out of him. Seeing that his companions had made it safely, Silver let out a fur-bristling howl from the other side of the river.

Tom looked toward the Beast, preparing himself for battle. Tagus was cantering toward them. The ground shook with every step.

Tom lowered his arm and swung the rope around in a tight circle. As Tagus approached, Tom steadied himself in Storm's saddle. When the Beast was twenty paces away, he stopped suddenly.

Tom looked at Tagus. He had seen a lot of terrifying things during the Beast Quest, but he had never seen such rage in a creature's eyes. Tom felt himself choke with fear.

Tagus charged. His muscular body surged toward Tom and Storm. His eyes narrowed in rage, Tagus kicked with his powerful front legs as he drew within striking distance.

Steeling himself, Tom flung the lasso at the charging Beast. It landed evenly around his neck, just above Malvel's enchanted collar. Now, Tom needed Storm's help to tighten the lasso around the Beast's neck, so it would hold fast. Tom didn't even need to flick the reins. Storm knew what to do, and bolted in the other direction, tugging the lasso securely into place.

Tagus let out a bellow of rage. His horse-body reared as the rope pulled tightly around his neck.

Chapter Eight

CHASE TO THE HILLS

STORM CHARGED ACROSS THE PRAIRIE. BUT
the rope wasn't very long — they couldn't keep
running.

"Stop, Storm!" Tom yelled, holding tightly on
to the lasso with one hand while tugging on his
horse's reins with the other. "Halt —"

But before his faithful horse could skid to a stop,
the rope was stretched taut and Tom was ripped
from Storm's back. Tom landed on the ground
with a sickening thud.

Before he even had a chance to think, the rope
in his hand jerked tight and Tom was being dragged
across the prairie. The ground tore at his skin and

clothes as he bounced roughly along the plain. Tagus was dragging him, but *where*?

Tom tried to hold on to the rope, but it was too difficult. With a powerful jerk, it was pulled from his hands. The sky was beginning to lighten, and the sounds of waking cattle could be heard across the plain.

Sitting up, Tom looked back toward the camp. The dark shape of the Beast loomed up again out of the mist. He paused for a moment, one foreleg impatiently beating the ground. Tagus reared, thrashing from side to side as he tried to free himself from the rope. His bellows of rage echoed over the plain. Tom could hear the cattle stirring. The noise must be frightening them.

Tom stood firmly, gripping his sword and matching the fierce gaze of Tagus. It was just him and the Beast on the wide-open prairie. Tom raised his sword and charged. Tagus did the same.

In the early morning light of the still prairie, Tom and the Beast ran at full speed toward each other. There was no way Tom could survive this. Tagus was five times his size and had ten times his strength. With just one swipe of the Beast's powerful arm, Tom would be knocked out cold.

But Tom had another plan. Just before the two met in a bloody collision, Tom slid to the ground. He went right under Tagus's thrashing hooves, grabbing the rope that trailed along on the ground.

Standing up, Tom now held the rope in his hand. Tagus pawed at the ground furiously. His eyes glared red with pure hate. Rearing up, the Beast charged again, this time with even more speed and anger.

Where was Storm? Tom wondered. It wasn't like his horse to abandon him. Without Storm's incredible speed, it would be much more difficult to defeat Tagus. What could he do?

Tom held his ground, staring Tagus down as he closed in. Just as the half man—half beast swung a deadly blow, Tom ducked.

This time, Tagus stopped in his tracks. Tom was now under the Beast's massive body. Holding tightly to the rope, Tom rolled himself out from under Tagus. The Beast reared again. Tom ran around the creature as quickly as he could. Tagus thrashed, but Tom was too quick. Before the Beast had a chance to recognize what was happening, Tom had wound the rope around his legs. Tagus wouldn't be able to take a step without falling.

Realizing this, the Beast stood still, but continued to bellow with rage.

This was his chance. Tom launched himself at Tagus. As he flew through the air, he let out a whoop of exhilaration. His heart thudded with a mixture of fear and excitement as he landed on the Beast's back. Tagus's strong muscles rippled beneath him.

But all Tom's strength wasn't enough to rein in the wild Beast. Another howl of fury escaped Tagus. His horse's body twisted and thrashed as he tried to escape the rope and throw Tom off. It was all Tom could do to stay on his back. The Beast swung his arms wildly. Tom ducked and slipped sideways; only his desperate grip on the rope stopped him from falling.

At last, with a fierce snort, Tagus braced himself and grabbed at the lasso around his neck. He tore at the rope, flexing his powerful arms. Tom's hands jerked backward as the tension in the rope gave way — it had snapped. Suddenly he had nothing to hold on to but the enchanted collar.

Tagus's human half twisted until he could look back at Tom. Tom caught a glimpse of his dark eyes blazing in the tangle of his hair. Then the Beast raised one arm and struck Tom a crushing blow on the side of the head.

→ Chapter Nine ←

Free!

Tom struggled to keep his grip on the collar. He blinked and shook his head, trying to drive away the dizzy feeling.

Tagus was stamping on the ground in a rage. Tom spotted something on the horizon. It was Storm! Elenna was riding him, and Silver ran alongside. They were coming to help.

As they approached, Tagus became even more agitated.

Tom called out to Elenna, "Spread out. We need to confuse him until I can get the collar off!"

They split up. Elenna rode Storm in front of the Beast, while Silver darted off to the side.

It was working! Tagus was confused. He paced from side to side, snorting and heaving. He didn't know who to go after first. This bought Tom enough time to pull out the key the good wizard, Aduro, had given him.

With one hand gripping the collar and one hand firmly holding the key, Tom grappled with the collar. But before Tom could get the key in the lock, Tagus gave one last stamp on the ground and stormed off, charging toward the hills. The threat of three foes had been enough to send him retreating.

With all his strength, Tom gripped the enchanted collar. He had to free Tagus!

Tom looked over his shoulder to see Elenna chasing after him on Storm. The Beast was moving too quickly for Tom to unlock the collar. It took all his strength just to hold on during the bumpy ride. He had to get Tagus to slow down. But how?

Tom looked toward his friend. Elenna gave him

a supportive nod and urged Storm into a gallop. Wind whipped through her hair as she raced after the Beast.

"Go, Storm!" Elenna yelled.

The black horse caught up with Tagus, pounding alongside him before he reached the slope that led to the plain where the herd was camped.

Tagus wheeled around and launched himself toward Elenna, his fur bristling with anger. He swung his arm wildly as they passed each other. Elenna ducked out of the way.

"Keep changing direction," Tom yelled to Elenna. "We need to tire him. I won't be able to get the collar off unless he slows down."

Tom watched as Elenna bent over the horse's neck, guiding him with her hands buried in his mane. "Storm! Come on, Storm!" she yelled in encouragement.

Silver darted around them, howling excitedly. Tom was terrified the wolf would be crushed under

the trampling hooves. The furious Tagus dodged one way and another as he charged at Elenna.

By now they had reached the river's edge. It was their last chance to stop Tagus before he crossed the river and scared the cattle into a stampede. *We can't keep this up forever!* Tom thought. What more could he do?

"Cut us off!" Tom yelled to his friend. "Get in between us and the river!"

Elenna kicked her heels, urging Storm to go faster, passing Tagus and cutting him off just before he reached the river. The Beast was forced to stop for just a moment. Tom used the opportunity to slip the key into the golden glowing collar. In a magical puff, it vanished from Tagus's neck.

Tagus let out a roar of fury as the collar disappeared. In that moment, Tom could feel all the Beast's anger — the horror of his enslavement to Malvel — being released.

It was over now.

→ Chapter Ten ←

North

"**W**E DID IT!" ELENNA CRIED. SHE BROUGHT Storm to a halt. The horse's sides were heaving after the long gallop. Elenna patted his sweating neck. "Well done, Storm," she said.

Silver let out a howl of triumph and stood panting, his tongue lolling out.

Tom slid from Tagus's back. On the ground, a crescent-shaped scrap of shining metal was lying next to one of the creature's hooves. A piece of Tagus's horseshoe!

"I know what that's for," Tom muttered, picking it up and thrusting it into his pocket.

Tom walked back to Storm, Silver, and Elenna.

Even though Tom knew the spell had been broken, he swallowed nervously as the Beast strode over to him.

For a moment, Tagus looked down at him. His dark eyes were calm now. He bowed his head majestically to Tom and Elenna. Then, looking up, he reached out with one hand to stroke Storm's nose.

Tom spotted movement in the shadow of a rock. A cougar was slinking down toward the herd.

Tagus's head swung around. He stamped his forehooves once, then took off across the river and after the predator. It fled, yelping in terror.

"Tagus can go back to what he's supposed to do," Tom said, watching as the magnificent Beast disappeared into the distance. Now Tagus would look after the people of Avantia; he wouldn't trouble them again.

Elenna nodded. "The herds will be safe."

"And the people of Dareton will have cattle to trade with the rest of the kingdom — they'll be able to rebuild the villages that were destroyed," Tom finished. He felt happiness flood him. But he still had one more thing to do. He pulled the crescent-shaped scrap of horseshoe out of his pocket and raised his shield. He could already see the place where this token would fit, beside the scale of Ferno the Fire Dragon, the piece of tooth from Sepron the Sea Serpent, and the tear of Cypher the Mountain Giant.

As he slotted the scrap into place, a sparkling mist curled around Tom's shoulders. He turned to see Aduro standing there. The wizard's outline was pale and shimmering in the morning light.

"Well done," Aduro said with a smile. "Thanks to your courage, another Beast is free."

Tom and Elenna glanced at each other. Elenna's eyes were shining at the wizard's praise, and Tom felt he could burst with pride.

"We did our best," he said.

"The whole of Avantia is in your debt," Aduro

told them. Pointing to Tom's shield, he added, "I see you found a piece of Tagus's horseshoe."

"Yes — what does it do?" Tom asked.

"From now on, you will be faster and more skillful in a fight," the wizard explained. "But take care. Use your power only for good."

"I will," said Tom.

"Where do we go now?" Elenna asked eagerly.

"Yes, what's next?" added Tom.

Aduro turned and pointed north. "You must go back the way you came," he said. "It is your task to meet a Beast among the snowy mountains. Tartok the Ice Beast is waiting for you to free her."

Tom looked to the horizon. In the far distance, he could see the white-tipped peaks of Avantia's northernmost mountains. He shivered as he imagined the icy winds and snowstorms that blew there all year round. He'd heard about Tartok. About the Beast's long yellow claws and fierce talons.

"What's the Beast doing now?" Tom asked

Aduro, without turning around. Aduro came to stand beside Tom.

"Destroying the great ice flats," Aduro said quietly. "Everyone there is in grave danger."

Tom felt his hand tighten around the handle of his sword, and he raised his shield up to his chest. "I'll save them," Tom said. "It's my Quest. I must complete it."

Aduro nodded. "You're more like your father than you know," said the wizard.

Elenna came to stand beside Tom. "We'll do it together," she said, placing a hand on Silver's head. Storm tossed his head and neighed. "We won't give up now."

"Then what are we waiting for?" Tom asked, grinning at his friends. "Let's go!"

"Avantia salutes you . . ." Aduro said, fading back into mist.

The four of them watched the wizard disappear. Then they began the long, cold trek north.